I0726529
LAS BRAVAS
PILAR

PILAR
A LAS BRAVAS STORY

INSPIRED BY THE AUDIO DRAMA AND THE WORK OF HISTORIAN IMMACULADA COLOMINA LIMONERO

INSPIRED BY THE AUDIO DRAMA LAS BRAVAS:PILAR
WRITTEN BY RICK RAPIER AND NICOLE NATALE
ILLUSTRATIONS BY ELLECK GURNARD DIBAKOANE

ISBN: 978-1-956146-58-5 (HARDCOVER)
ISBN: 978-1-956146-59-2 (PAPERBACK)
ISBN: 978-1-956146-60-8 (E-BOOK)

HAS IT REALLY BEEN SO LONG? SO MANY DECADES SINCE LOSING SUCH WOMEN, SUCH DEAR FRIENDS?

"WOULD YOU LIKE ANOTHER CAFÉ?"

"NO... PLEASE LEAVE ME TO MY MEMORIES, YOUNG MAN..."

MY MIND WAS BACK IN MADRID... 1936... MERE MONTHS AFTER THE CIVIL WAR HAD BEEN THRUST UPON US.
I WAS THINKING OF PILAR... AND HOW HER HUSBAND HAD BEEN CALLED TO WAR, LEAVING HER ALONE...

PILAR WAS LEFT ALONE TO FEND FOR HER TWINS AND HER SISTER LINA'S TODDLER SON CRUZ...
...MENDING CLOTHES AS IF LIFE WAS NORMAL.

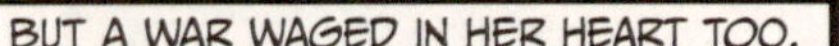

BUT A WAR WAGED IN HER HEART TOO.

AS THE BATTLE DREW NEARER TO MADRID AND HER HOME...

... WHEN SHOULD SHE AND THE CHILDREN LEAVE THE CITY? AND TO WHERE SHOULD THEY GO??

SUCH THOUGHTS HAD TO WAIT. LEAVING THE BABY FOR HER NEIGHBOR INES TO LOOK AFTER, PILAR HEADED DEEPER INTO MADRID TO DELIVER A PARTY DRESS TO LA DOÑA, A WEALTHY WOMAN.

"PILAR, DEAR, YOUR WORK IS EXQUISITE AS EVER..."

"... BUT I'VE NO MONEY TO PAY YOU."

"YOU SHOULD NOT HAVE COME TODAY. BUT LET ME GIVE YOU THESE COOKIES FOR YOUR CHILDREN."

IN THOSE DAYS, I WAS KNOWN AS 'LA BLONDE'...
... A PHOTOJOURNALIST BY TRADE.

"MAY I TAKE YOUR PICTURE, SEÑORITA?"

"I'M MARRIED. BUT WHY TAKE MY PHOTO??"

IT WAS A TIME OF SPANIARD AGAINST SPANIARD, SO TRUST WAS HARD TO FIND. SUSPICIOUS OF MY MOTIVES, PILAR QUICKLY GOT OFF THE BUS. I EXPECTED TO NEVER SEE HER AGAIN. I WAS WRONG.

SHE WOULD LATER TELL ME SHE REGRETTED HER DECISION AS SHE SOON FACED THE TURRET OF A TANK DRIVEN BY THE FORCES OF THE FASCIST GENERAL FRANCO...

... AND HOW SHE RAN ALL THE WAY HOME, HER HEART POUNDING.

BUT WHEN SHE RETURNED HOME...
KNOCK!
KNOCK!
KNOCK!

AN ANGRY INES SCOLDED HER FOR NOT RECLAIMING CRUZ ON TIME.

"I'M SO SORRY, INES. THANK YOU!"

SHE TOLD INES THE FASCISTS WERE HEADED THEIR WAY...

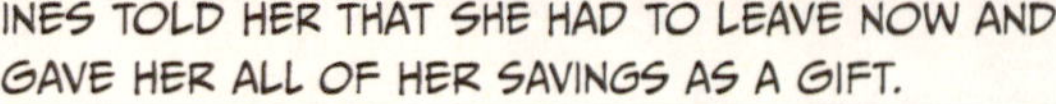
INES TOLD HER THAT SHE HAD TO LEAVE NOW AND GAVE HER ALL OF HER SAVINGS AS A GIFT.

THIS GENEROUS ACT HAPPENED NONE TOO SOON, AS THE FASCISTS INVADED THEIR NEIGHBORHOOD!
BAM!
BAM!

PEW!
PEW!

AND INES WAS SHOT AND KILLED RIGHT IN FRONT OF POOR PILAR AND THE FRIGHTENED CHILDREN.

ONLY TO BE FOLLOWED BY BOMBS RAINING DOWN FROM ABOVE, DESTROYING THEIR HOMES!

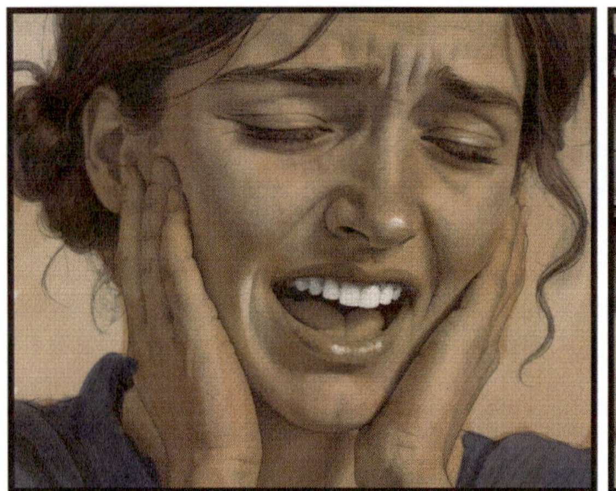

WITH A PROMISE FROM NEIGHBORS TO TELL HER HUSBAND THEY HAD GONE INTO MADRID TO FIND PILAR'S MILICIANA SISTER LINA, PILAR AND THE CHILDREN SET OUT ON FOOT.

MEANWHILE, TO THE NORTH, HER SISTER LINA REQUESTED LEAVE TO GO SEE HER SON.

"COMRADE CAPTAIN, MY SON IS WITH MY SISTER..."

"... I CLAIM MY RIGHT TO GO SEE HIM!"

WITH HER CHILDREN MATEO AND CARMEN, PILAR JOINED THOUSANDS WHO ALSO FLED THE FIGHTING.

"I AM NOT A DESERTER! I HAVE A RIGHT TO SEE MY LITTLE BOY!"
LINA FACED TRIALS OF HER OWN AS SHE SOUGHT HELP FROM OTHER UNITS TO REACH MADRID.

UNFORTUNATELY, DESPERATION TURNED PEOPLE TO THEIR WORST IMPULSES, MAKING EVEN PEACEFUL MADRID A PLACE OF UNFORESEEN DANGERS...

"GIVE ME ALL YOUR MONEY, LADY! NOW!!!"

"DROP THAT KNIFE, CREEP!!"

"THIS AIN'T OVER — I'LL BE BACK!"

"YOU CAN CALL ME 'LA BLONDE.'"

IN A BORROWED TRUCK, LINA DROVE INTO MADRID...

BUT BEFORE SHE COULD REACH HER APARTMENT, A BOMB EXPLODED, STOPPING HER COLD.

I HELPED PILAR FIND HER SISTER'S APARTMENT BUILDING AND THERE THEY WAITED UNTIL...

MORE DESTRUCTION FELL FROM FASCIST BOMBER PLANES OVERHEAD.

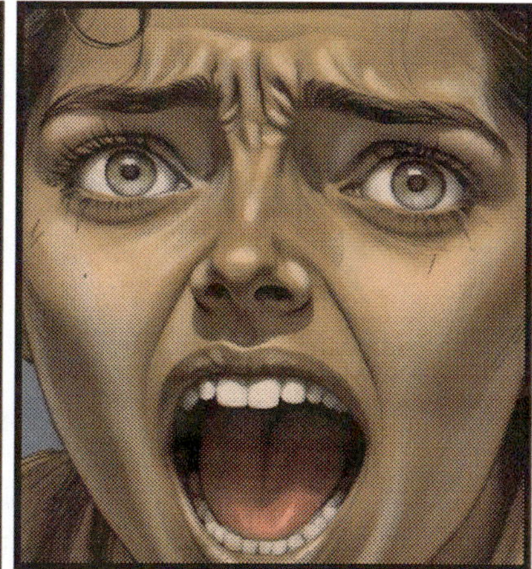

"EVERYONE!!! INTO THE SUBWAY!!!"

WITH BOMB BLASTS EVERY FEW MINUTES, IT WAS A TERRIFYING EXPERIENCE FOR EVERYONE.

WHAT PILAR DIDN'T REALIZE WAS THAT ESCAPE INTO THE SUBWAY INTRODUCED HER TO LIFELONG FRIENDS WHO WOULD HELP IN HER IN DRAMATIC AND UNEXPECTED WAYS.

AS LINA MADE HER WAY THROUGH THE CITY TO HER APARTMENT BUILDING, HER ANGER WITH FRANCO AND HER LOVE FOR HER LITTLE BOY CRUZ DROVE HER ONWARD THROUGH THE RUBBLE.

AFTER SEARCHING THE NEIGHBORHOOD A BIT FOR HER SISTER AND SON, LINA DECIDED TO WAIT IN HER APARTMENT. THE STRESS OF WAR LED HER TO HAVE TOO MUCH RED WINE AND SHE PASSED OUT.

WITH WINE IN HER HEAD AND THE LOUD RADIO IN HER EARS, SHE COULDN'T HEAR PILAR KNOCKING AT THE DOOR...

BUT AIR RAID SIRENS BLARED AND BOMBS BEGAN TO FALL ON THE CITY ONCE AGAIN!

SENDING PILAR AND THE CHILDREN BACK INTO THE STREETS.

BUT IT WAS ENOUGH TO WAKE EVEN THE DEAD.

IN THE CHAOS THAT FELL, CRUZ WAS TORN FROM PILAR'S ARMS! IT WAS YOUNG CARMEN WHO BRAVELY CHASED HIM DOWN AND TOOK THE BOY IN HER ARMS...

... JUST AS A MISSILE CRATERED THE STREET AND SHREDDED THE FRAGILE HUMAN SHIELD SHE MADE OF HER OWN BODY...

... WHICH LINA WITNESSED.

ALL OF MADRID SEEMED TO ECHO WITH HER MOURNFUL WAIL AS PILAR CRIED OUT IN SHEER ANGUISH.

BACK AT LINA'S APARTMENT, PILAR HEARD A RADIO REPORT THAT MEXICO WAS EVACUATING SPANISH CHILDREN TO RESCUE THEM FROM THE WAR...

SHE KNEW WHAT SHE HAD TO DO —

GET HER SON MATEO ON THAT SHIP.

AFTER SKIRTING AN ANGRY MOB OF PARENTS WHO MISSED THE LAST TRANSPORT TO THE COAST...

...PILAR GAINED THE HELP OF HER SUBWAY FRIENDS WHO AGREED TO TAKE HER TO BARCELONA.

BUT ALONG THE WAY, THE CAR BROKE DOWN...

... FORCING PILAR & MATEO TO HITCHHIKE.

JUST WHEN SHE THOUGHT SHE HAD MADE IT, THE TRUCK DRIVER DECIDED HE WANTED SOMETHING IN EXCHANGE FOR THE RIDE: "I SCRATCH YOUR BACK... YOU SCRATCH MINE, BABY..."

IT WAS THE LAST STRAW FOR A WOMAN — A MOTHER — PUSHED TOO FAR.

"HEY, WHAT'S WITH THAT KNIFE, LADY?"

"AAARGH! QUIT STABBING ME!!"

"WE'RE GONNA CRASH!"

HE WAS DEAD... BUT HE BROUGHT IT UPON HIMSELF.

PILAR & HER SON WALKED TO A CLINIC WHERE THEY WERE TREATED...

... BY MISSIONARY VOLUNTEERS OF SWISS CHARITY AYUDA SUIZA AND DRIVEN TO THE PORT OF BARCELONA SO THAT MATEO COULD SAIL TO MEXICO.

THOUGH THE WAR WOULD WAGE ON FOR ANOTHER 3 YEARS, AND, THANK GOD, PILAR WOULD SURVIVE IT... AT LEAST LITTLE MATEO WOULD NO LONGER HAVE TO SUFFER THE HORRORS OF WAR.

"MAMA? I WON'T BE AFRAID IN MEXICO... KNOW WHY?"

"WHY, MATEO??"
"'CUZ I'M GOING TO BE JUST AS BRAVE... AS YOU!"

SUCH MEMORIES OFTEN RETURN TO ME, STORIES OF BRAVE WOMEN WHOM HISTORY BOOKS SO OFTEN OVERLOOKED. THEY SAY HISTORY IS WRITTEN BY ITS VICTORS... BUT AS FOR ME, SOMEONE WHO LIVED IT, I SAY, "IT IS WRITTEN BY ITS SURVIVORS -- LAS BRAVAS!!"